GLORIA GOES TO GAY PRIDE

GLORIA GOES TO GAY PRIDE

by Lesléa Newman • Illustrated by Russell Crocker

Alyson Wonderland
an imprint of Alyson Publications, Inc.

Other books by Lesléa Newman

Books for children:
Heather Has Two Mommies

Books for adults:
Just Looking For My Shoes
Good Enough To Eat
Love Me Like You Mean It
A Letter To Harvey Milk
Bubbe Meisehs by Shayneh Maidelehs
Secrets
Sweet Dark Places

Typeset and printed in the United States of America.

This is an Alyson Wonderland book
from Alyson Publications, Inc., 40 Plympton St., Boston, Mass. 02118.
Distributed in England by GMP Publishers, P.O. Box 247, London N17 9QR England.

First edition, first printing: June 1991

5 4 3 2 1

ISBN 1-55583-185-0

For Asha and Ishana

Holidays are lots of fun. On Valentine's Day, I give Mama Grace candy and Mama Rose flowers and they give me a big card shaped like a heart that says GLORIA, WE LOVE YOU.

On Halloween, we go trick-or-treating. I get dressed up like a cowgirl and Butterscotch wears a red bandana around her neck. Mama Grace dresses up like an astronaut and Mama Rose dresses up like a clown.

On *Chanukah*, we light the *menorah* and play spin-the-*draydl* and eat *latkes*. I like my *latkes* with applesauce. Mama Rose likes her *latkes* with sour cream. Mama Grace likes her *latkes* plain.

On Mothers' Day, I make my two mommies breakfast in bed. Butterscotch helps me cook. Mama Rose and Mama Grace say I make the best peanut-butter-and-jelly sandwiches in the whole wide world.

But today is a special holiday. Today is Gay Pride Day, and I get to be in a parade!

I get up early and run downstairs. Mama Grace and Mama Rose have already finished their breakfast. They're down on their hands and knees on the living room floor making signs for the parade with crayons and paints and magic markers.

9

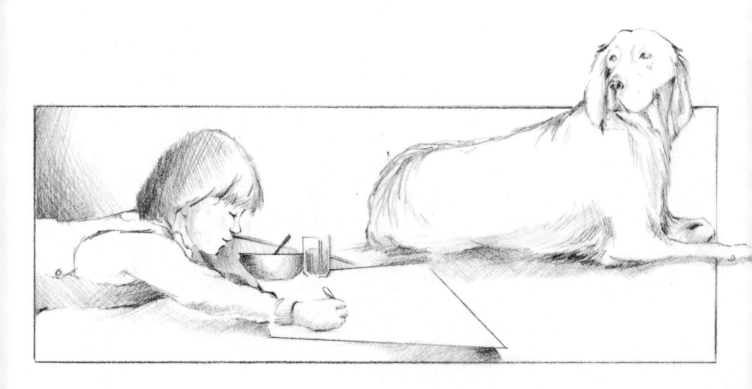

I want to make a sign, too. I eat my cereal and drink my juice as fast as I can.

Then I read Mama Grace's sign

11

and Mama Rose's sign

and then I make my sign.

After we finish our signs, it's time to go to the Gay Pride Parade. Mama Rose ties my sign on my back with a big purple string so everyone can read it. Mama Grace ties a big purple bow around Butterscotch's neck. We put our lunch in Mama Grace's big knapsack and then off we go to the parade!

14

The sun is shining and lots of people are going to the parade. I see a mommy with two babies in a stroller and a man with three dogs on a leash.

15

Soon we get to the schoolyard where the parade starts. Lots of people are there. "Hi, Andrea," I wave to our mail carrier, and she waves back.

"Hi, Gloria." My music teacher comes up behind us and gives me a purple balloon.

"Guess who?" Someone puts their hands over my eyes. It's Richard, the nurse who works at the hospital with Mama Grace. Richard is marching with his son, Jonathan.

Soon we line up to march. We stand right next to a band with drummers and horn players and baton twirlers. Mama Grace reaches into her knapsack and pulls out a tambourine so I can be part of the band, too.

19

Now the drummers start drumming and the twirlers start twirling and off we go! Mama Rose and Mama Grace hold hands and I hold Mama Grace's hand. Usually my mommies don't hold hands when we go out, but today they do because today is Gay Pride Day, and that makes them smile.

We march right up Main Street, past Koppel's Shoes, where I got my new red sneakers. Mr. Koppel comes out and waves to us. I wave my tambourine and Butterscotch wags her tail.

Next we pass Angelina's Home Cooking, where we eat supper sometimes. Angelina stands outside with her apron on, waving her big wooden spoon.

When we get near the park, everyone starts clapping and singing: "Two-four-six-eight, being gay is really *great!*" The people standing on the sidewalk clap and sing with us. They smile when we pass.

But right next to the park, some people aren't singing or clapping. They stand very quietly on the sidewalk next to a sign.

24

When we get next to them, Butterscotch starts to growl. "Hush," Mama Rose says to Butterscotch. "They won't hurt us."

I pull at Mama Grace's sleeve. "Why do they want us to go away?" I ask. "Some people think Mama Rose and I shouldn't love each other," Mama Grace says. I don't understand. "But you always tell me love is the most important thing of all."

Mama Rose picks me up. "Love *is* the most important thing of all," she says. "Some women love women, some men love men, and some women and men love each other. That's why we march in the parade — so everyone can have a choice."

26

When we get in front of the park, Mama Grace tells me to look up. I see a thousand balloons in the sky! Red and orange and yellow and green and purple and blue balloons, just like a rainbow! We march right under them, into the park.

27

A band is playing music and everyone starts to dance.

Soon we sit down on the grass to eat our lunch. Jonathan and Richard sit down with us.

Jonathan and I make daisy chains and play catch with his beach ball while Mama Rose and Mama Grace and Richard listen to all the speeches.

After the speeches, we walk around the park. There are t-shirts and buttons and books and newspapers and lots of other things to buy.

My mommies buy me a white t-shirt with a picture of all the balloons on it.

Then they buy each other presents. Mama Grace buys Mama Rose a necklace made of seashells. Mama Rose buys Mama Grace a purple baseball cap with a pink triangle on it.

We put on our new presents and then we go get ice cream cones.

When it's time to go home, Mama Rose and Mama Grace hold hands as we walk to the rainbow of balloons.

I look at my mommies and I feel happy because we had so much fun. I wish we didn't have to wait another whole year for Gay Pride Day to come again.

About the author:

Lesléa Newman lives in western Massachusetts, where she writes books for children and adults, teaches women's writing workshops, and, once a year, celebrates Gay Pride Day.

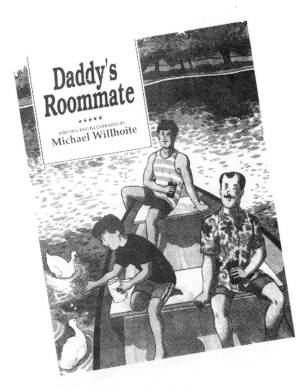

turist Michael Willhoite, are simple and colorful, and the binding is sturdy — perfect for children aged two to five.

• "*Daddy's Roommate*, delightfully illustrated by Willhoite, presents the peanut-butter-and-jelly pleasures of daily life after Daddy divorces Mommy and starts living with Frank. Kids will love the detailed depictions of catching bugs for show-and-tell, Frank and Daddy shaving together, and trips to the zoo." — *New York Native*

• "An upbeat, positive portrayal of a situation common to many children with gay fathers." — *Booklist*

• "This picture book is an auspicious beginning to the Alyson Wonderland imprint. Willhoite's text is suitably straightforward, and the format — single lines of copy beneath full-page illustrations — easily accessible to the intended audience. The colorful characters with their contemporary ward-

robes and familiar surroundings lend the tale a stabilizing air of warmth and familiarity." — *Publishers Weekly*

• "For the younger child who has coped with a divorce, and now spends part of his time with his gay father and companion, the story offers reasssurance. And it doesn't try to skirt the issue: Dad and his roommate are shown hugging, although there is nothing sexually explicit. Rating: two stars." — *Detroit Free Press*

• "This is a bright book, full of color illustrations by the author, and designed to appeal to young audiences. This book is a great one for kids with gay or lesbian family members." — *Update*

HOW WOULD YOU FEEL IF YOUR DAD WAS GAY?, by Ann Heron and Meredith Maran; illustrated by Kris Kovick, cloth, $10.00. Jasmine,

Michael, and Noah are all regular kids except for one thing: They have gay parents. They have some unique concerns that they've never seen discussed by anyone else. This book, written by two lesbian mothers with help from their sons, will be a lifeline for other young people who face the same issues. It will also help their classmates, teachers, and parents to better understand just how varied today's families can be.

FAMILIES, by Michael Willhoite, $3.00. Many kinds of families, including a diversity of races, generations, and cultural backgrounds, are depicted in this coloring book (which is accompanied by a short text); several of the families include lesbian or gay parents. Ages 2–6.

SUPPORT YOUR LOCAL BOOKSTORE

Most of the books described above are available at your nearest gay or feminist bookstore, and many of them will be available at other bookstores. If you can't get these books locally, order by mail using this form.

Enclosed is $_____ for the following books. (Add $1.00 postage when ordering just one book. If you order two or more, we'll pay the postage.)

1. _____

2. _____

3. _____

name: _____ address: _____

city: _____ state: _____ zip: _____

ALYSON PUBLICATIONS
Dept. H-85, 40 Plympton St., Boston, MA 02118

After December 31, 1992, please write for current catalog.